A JOLLY CHRISTMAS
AT THE PATTERPRINTS

A·JOLLY·CHRISTMAS AT·THE·PATTERPRINTS

TOLD BY
VERA NYCE

PICTURES BY
HELENE NYCE

Parents' Magazine Press ⋎ New York

Through a happenstance we discovered this Christmas picture book, written and illustrated over fifty years ago but never published. The author and artist were probably best known for their Flossie Fisher's Funnies *which ran as a regular feature in the* Ladies' Home Journal *prior to 1915. Vera Nyce wrote the stories and poems, and her daughter Helene did the silhouette drawings. The Flossie Fisher Club for children was known around the world, and the Flossie Fisher characters were duplicated in enameled jewelry and on china.*

The club was discontinued during World War I since the jewelry and other items distributed to the members were manufactured in Germany. Helene Nyce then went on to become well known for her work in magazine art and advertising.

A charming example of the art and writing of the early part of the century, A Jolly Christmas at the Patterprints *should entertain children of the 1970s—and also provide a fascinating look at the kind of picture book that perhaps their grandparents enjoyed.*

The Editors

Now the way we heard this story was from old Lije Herringbone, the tramp rat. We had just settled down for a quiet Christmas afternoon rest when in he came, stuffed to the neck with plum pudding. He was so excited he could scarcely get the words out, telling us about the doings at Peter and Jemima Patterprint's house, and how he came to spend Christmas with them.

Such a time they had there, I'm only sorry I couldn't have joined in myself, but I'll do my best to tell you about it.

Well, this is the way it happened. Peter Patterprint was sitting by the fireplace trotting Pitty on one knee and Patty on the other. The baby was asleep in his cunning wee cradle. And Jemima was humming quietly to herself as she stirred the soup that had just been hung over the fire. While little Peggy clung to her apron and caught her breath at every sound.

This was Christmas Eve, and there was great excitement in the house of Patterprint.

All at once there was the most terrible clattering on the tiny back porch, and a frantic fumbling of the door latch. And before Peter could lift the frightened babies to the floor, *bang* the door crashed open, and Lije Herringbone and a flurry of snow came whirling into the room together. Poor old Lije was so frightened he could scarcely speak.

"Whatever is the matter with you, Lije Herringbone?" sharply demanded Jemima Patterprint. "I declare it is enough to scare a body out of a year's growth! Can't you see the baby's asleep? And poor little Peggy trembling from head to foot!"

"Oh, Mrs. Patterprint, if you'd only been there!" gasped Lije. Then he paused a minute. "My, but it does smell good in here."

"Do go on, Lije," said Jemima impatiently.

"Well, I was coming through the woods," said Lije, "and suddenly I heard something thrashing 'mongst the bushes, and there was Santa Claus all tangled up! His pack and his sleigh and everything. Then when he got himself untangled, he just hopped on that sleigh and coasted down the wood road like the wind. I took a shortcut and

commenced to run. Folks do say Santa Claus won't hurt anyone, but I don't know—I never saw a mouse with a white beard before. I was scared out my wits and nigh into fits, and I just peppered through those woods up to your door."

"Why Lije, how you do talk!" laughed Jemima. And Peter and the babies joined in the laughter, too. "You know that Santa wouldn't hurt a hair of anyone's head!"

"But if he's that close, Jemima," said Peter, "these children should be hustled into bed, and spry about it, too. First thing you know he'll be here and surprise us, and then"—he paused—"nothing but switches in their stockings."

"You're right, Pa," Jemima said. "Now you get the old blankets and a quilt for Lije. It's getting too late for him to be trailing around through the snow, and after he's had a bit of soup he can sleep on the sofa. Meantime, I'll take care of the children."

You may believe that Lije was glad and thankful for Jemima's kind invitation. He didn't want to run into Santa Claus again. No indeed! He felt far safer in the house, for no telling what might happen alone in the woods with Santa. Foolish old Lije! But then he was just a poor old tramp rat and didn't really know much about these things, for he had never had a Christmas before.

So Jemima fed the children and got them tucked down for the night. But what with all the excitement of Christmas Eve, it was quite some time before the squeaking little Patterprints were sound asleep.

Meantime, Lije stirred the soup vigorously and tasted it even more vigorously. The soup was good and he was very hungry. Indeed, he had time to make quite a supper before Peter and Jemima came tiptoeing from the bedroom.

"Now," said Jemima as she bustled up to the fireplace. "Give me that spoon, Lije, and Peter, do you stir up the fire, for this soup is scarcely warm, and we must have supper before Santa—" But before she could finish, there came such a pitter, patter—scrape—rumblety BUMBLETY noise in the chimney. "Oh, Peter, Peter, there's Santa now! Lije, grab the kettle, quick! Peter—Help!"

But that's as far as she got, for with a mighty splash, down the

chimney came Santa and landed right in the soup! Oh, horrible thought!

What a dreadful time there was to be sure! Lije tumbled himself and his stool over backward. He squealed at the top of his voice, "Oh, oh, Santa's in the soup. He's drowning right before my eyes, and it's all my fault, too. Oh, oh, whatever shall we do!" And he sobbed and moaned into his ragged red handkerchief.

"Do!" exclaimed Santa angrily. "Why, help me out of this, of course. Not much use sitting there and crying. My heavens, I never had such a thing happen in all my life! The disgrace of it!" And poor Santa groaned as he floundered about in the soup, for it was uncomfortably warm.

Jemima knew that something had to be done—and quickly, too. "There, there, Santa," she said soothingly. "We'll have you out in the shake of a mouse's tail." She hooked her wooden spoon into Santa's collar, and she and Peter gave a long pull and a strong pull. With that, Santa and a good part of the soup came splashing onto the floor. Santa scolded and stamped, and Lije wept, until Jemima begged them to stop else they'd wake the children.

"I'm sure it's enough to put anyone out," exclaimed Santa. "Here's my very best coat—finished only this morning—completely ruined! What will Mrs. Claus say to that, I wonder? Never heard of anyone having soup on Christmas Eve anyway."

"I didn't know Santa had a temper," thought poor flustered Jemima as she mopped the soup off the floor. "I thought he'd have more patience."

"This is an awful thing to happen!" fumed Santa again. "There's my pack in the bottom of that soup, and if you don't get it out you'll have no presents *this* Christmas."

Then Lije dried his tears in a hurry. He hustled to take one side of the kettle and Peter took the handle on the other side. Between them they carried it to the yard and drained off the soup. Lije groaned at the wicked waste as the soup ran over the snow, but he brightened when he found that Santa's pack was well covered with oilcloth.

Meantime, Jemima stripped Santa of his coat and gave it a regular tubbing. Lucky for him he wore great long rubber boots. Then she spread it before the fire to dry.

Now when Santa saw that his coat was not quite spoiled and that the Patterprints were doing all they could to help, his good humor was quite restored. He chuckled as he said, "You good people scurry off to bed as quickly as you can. You have no time to eat now. But you can eat supper and breakfast in one after I've gone. No peeping, mind," he added with a wink, "or I'll put switches in all your stockings."

So the green sofa was rolled over to one side, and Lije was made comfortable with blankets and a quilt. Before getting into bed he pinned one of his socks to the quilt. It had a great hole in the toe but Lije didn't mind that. Then he crept between the blankets and commenced to peep as hard as he could.

Santa was in a great hurry so he might not have noticed this, but suddenly Lije became excited and shouted, "Oh say, Santa, put in lots of things to make a noise, will you?"

Santa turned around and stared at him so sternly that Lije shut his eyes—right straight! Then Santa went back to his work. "Lucky thing I have a waterproof sack," he said to himself. "Soup wouldn't improve some of these presents."

Santa stuffed six pair of new socks and a beautiful spotted handkerchief into Lije's stocking, along with a pink popcorn ball and some candy. Then he took his coat from before the fire and shook his head. It was still quite damp. "I'm afraid I'll have to trouble you, Lije," he whispered with a mischievous smile, and he twitched the patchwork quilt from off the bed. "It's too cold to walk in icicles," he continued, "and that's what my coat will be in two minutes."

He folded the quilt over his shoulders shawl fashion, and trotted out through the doorway. He really couldn't go back up the chimney, for the fire had been blazed up to dry his coat, and not being used to doors he left this one wide open.

Wheee-ee-ee, *Wheee-ee-ee* went the wind as it whistled round the corners of the little house, right into the open doorway and under Lije's blanket. He shivered and woke with a jump. Then he gave two more jumps—one to close the door and the other over to the fireplace. He poked up the fire to give him enough light so that he could peek into other folks' stockings before they were out of bed.

But at the sight of his own stuffed sock, he gave such a joyful squeak that the whole family came tumbling into the room. The little Patterprints rubbed their eyes, but no one can remain sleepy over a Christmas stocking for very long. The room soon echoed with squeaks

of merriment. Lije was delighted with his new socks and spotted handkerchief, and the pink popcorn ball was most lovely. He was especially fond of popcorn balls. "I'll never be afraid of Santa again," he said laughing.

Peter Patterprint had slippers with big red roses on them, a year's subscription to *The Daily Nibbler* and a new almanac. Jemima had a silver thimble and a darning egg, a china tea set and a new rolling pin. As for the children, they had picture books and toys and goodies of all sorts. Of course everyone ate too much candy, so no one wanted breakfast, but instead, they had an early dinner, and such a dinner it was!

Lije was the life of the party, pattering around in his new socks and trying to help and getting in everyone's way. But they all forgave him because he meant well and because it was Christmas. He kept the little Patterprints happy while their mother fussed in the kitchen, telling them jokes and riddles and playing blind man's buff and roasting chestnuts in the fire.

Soon the table was set with all sorts of good things to eat—acorn pudding, nut patties with gooseberry jam, wheat and barley cutlets and much, much more.

After feasting on all the fine food Jemima had prepared, it was time for the plum pudding. Before anyone could stop him, Lije rushed into the kitchen to bring it out himself. It smelled so good he couldn't help but pick off a bit and pop it into his mouth. But it was so hot that he burned his fingers and tongue. This made him jump and he almost unbalanced the platter with that lovely pudding on it. Fortunately, he caught it just in time, although he gave everyone quite a scare. Jemima did make such good plum pudding it would have been a shame if it had landed on the floor.

In spite of all the eating they had done, they managed to finish off the pudding, and Lije even had a second helping.

And that's the story Lije told us of the jolly Christmas he had with the Patterprints, and I believe every word of it!

The End